HAYSTACK

BONNIE and ARTHUR GEISERT

HOUGHTON MIFFLIN COMPANY BOSTON

For our parents

Walter Lorraine 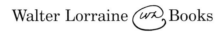 Books

Text copyright © 1995 by Bonnie Geisert
Illustrations copyright © 1995 by Arthur Geisert

www.houghtonmifflinbooks.com

Geisert, Bonnie.
    Haystack / by Bonnie Geisert and Arthur Geisert.
        p. cm.
    RNF ISBN 0-395-69722-0   PA ISBN 0-618-33522-6
    1. Hay—Juvenile literature. 2. Stacks (Hay, grain, etc.)—
Juvenile literature. 3. Hay as feed—Juvenile literature.
[1. Hay. 2. Farm life.] I. Geisert, Arthur. II. Title.
SB198.g45   1995
633.2'086—dc20   94-7684
                                                         CIP
                                                         AC

Manufactured in China
SCP 10 9 8 7 6 5 4 3 2

HAYSTACK

In a time not so long ago, before machines made hay in convenient bundles, haystacks stood high, long, and wide on the prairie.

Across the prairie in the spring, the grass grew tall.

When the grass in the hay field was ready, the farmer hooked the mower to the tractor and cut swath after swath around the field.

After drying, the grass was rolled into windrows with a hay rake.

The hydraulic lift with its hay basket was attached to the tractor
and the windrows were bunched into piles.

Pile after pile was brought to the center of the field, where a frame
was built for the haystack.

The haystack grew quickly.

Everyone in the family helped. The hay was spread evenly with pitchforks.

As the haystack grew higher, tromping packed the hay
so that the whole field would fit.

There was time to rest while waiting for the loads of hay.

When the last hay from the field was collected, the haystack was done.

It was a very large stack of hay.

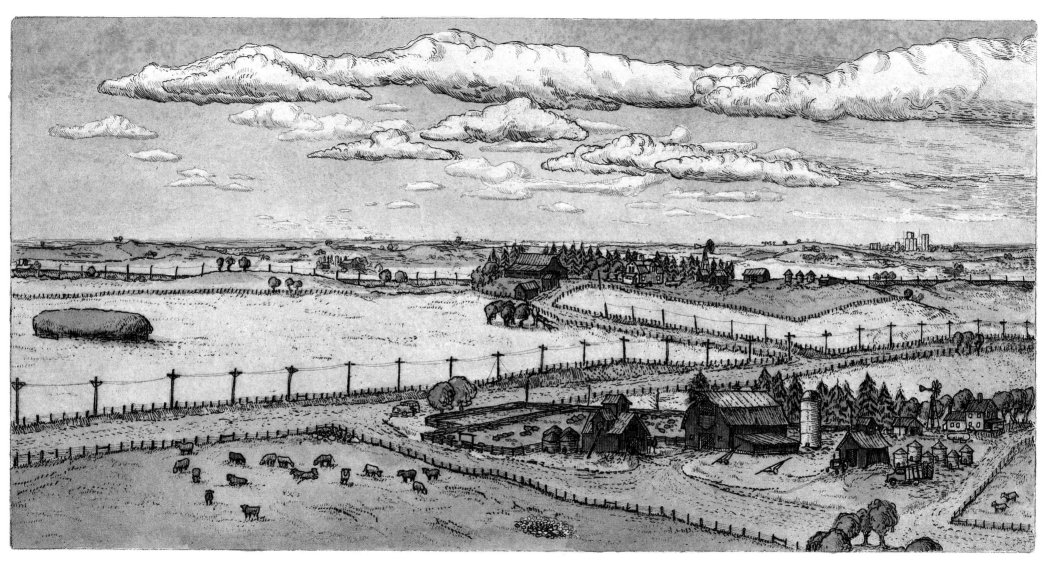

It would feed the cattle for the rest of the year.

Thunderstorms threatened the haystack.

If hit by lightning, the haystack could catch fire and burn to the ground.

On hot days, the haystack shaded the cattle from the sun.

The cattle ate as far as they could reach. Then, the hay was
pitched down to them.

Before winter, the frame was removed.

Now the cattle could reach the hay.

They stayed close to the haystack through the winter.

They were protected from the cold winter wind and they had food whenever they wanted.

Near the end of winter, when it was time for the calves to be born,
the cattle were herded to another field.

The pigs and their piglets were moved to the hay field.

Now they had the field to run in.

And they had the food from the haystack.

The haystack was a place to feed and a place to rest.

After some weeks, the cattle and new calves were herded back into the hay field. They shared the last of the hay with the pigs.

After the months of feeding and sheltering the livestock, all that was left of the haystack was a heap of manure.

The manure was pitched into the spreader and spread over the field as food for the grass.

And the grass grew tall in preparation for the cycle to begin again.